DELILAH

Other Avon Flare Books by
Bruce and Carole Hart

SOONER OR LATER
WAITING GAMES

CAROLE HART was one of the original writers for "Sesame Street," for which she won an Emmy Award in 1970. She also helped put together the Marlo Thomas special "Free to Be You and Me." Like Delilah, Carole Hart lives on Manhattan's Upper West Side. She is married to Bruce Hart, with whom she often collaborates on many film and book projects.

2740

DELILAH

Carole Hart

Illustrations by Edward Frascino

AN AVON  CAMELOT BOOK

4th grade reading level has been determined by using the Fry Readability Scale.

AVON BOOKS
A division of
The Hearst Corporation
959 Eighth Avenue
New York, New York 10019

Text Copyright © 1973 by Carole Hart
Illustrations Copyright © 1973 by Edward Frascino
Published by arrangement with Harper & Row, Publishers, Inc.
Library of Congress Catalog Card Number: 82-18433
ISBN: 0-380-62729-9

Library of Congress Cataloging in Publication Data

Hart, Carole.
  Delilah.

  (An Avon/Camelot book)
  Summary: Ten-year-old Delilah plays basketball with the
garbageman, sings with a band in the park, cries when
her parents fight, and generally enjoys her life.
  [1. Family life—Fiction] I. Frascino, Edward, ill.
II. Title
PZ7.H25629De 1983   [Fic]   82-18433
ISBN 0-380-62729-9

First Camelot Printing, March, 1983

Printed in the U.S.A.

DON 10 9 8 7 6 5 4 3 2 1

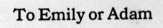

To Emily or Adam

Delilah Bush is almost ten years old.

She's the tallest girl in her class.

She plays basketball and drums.

She has two left feet. (They're made of green felt, and they're sewn to the seat of her favorite pair of blue jeans.)

She also has short, very curly, brownish-red in winter, reddish-brown in summer hair that frames her face.

One of Delilah's eyes is gray. The other is gray-green.

She is named Delilah because her mother and father were young and silly at the time she was born.

Bounce.

Delilah was dribbling her basketball to the playground down the street.

Bounce.

She felt light, as if she were riding on a soft sighing wind.

Bounce.

She didn't have a care in the world.

Oof.

She rode right into a garbage man.

"Shee . . ." he said.

"Sorry," she said.

"No mind," he said.

Then he grabbed her basketball. And he started dribbling it down the street. Fast.

"Hey!" she said.

And she ran after him, feeling slow, and wondering, *Where did the wind go?*

He stopped in the playground.

She caught up to him.

He smiled.

She breathed hard and tried not to show it.

"You wanna play ball?" he asked.

"Sure," she answered. "Let's have a free-throw contest."

That's what she did best.

She got seven out of ten baskets and won the first round.

He got six.

The next time they tied. Eight baskets apiece.

"Let's try lay-ups," he said.

"No," she said.

"Why not?" he asked.

"I'm not very good at lay-ups," she said, softly.

"What?" he said.

"I'm not very good at lay-ups," she said, a little louder.

"I can't hear you," he said.

"I'm not very good at lay-ups," she shouted.

"Well," he said, "if you keep telling yourself you're not any good at lay-ups, you'll never get any better."

He laughed and threw her the basketball.

"Try one. Let's see."

She charged down the court, and missed—by a mile.

"No wonder you're no good. You move like a hurricane. Take it easy. Pretend you're riding on a soft sighing wind."

And he showed her.

Nice and slow and graceful like a dance step.

She tried it his way.

It worked.

She tried it again.

And again.

It felt good.

She might have played forever.

But a loud and awful horn started honking.

"That's for me," he said.

So they walked back up the street together to his garbage truck.

Behind it there was an old man in a car, leaning on his horn.

"What do you think you're doing, leaving a garbage truck in the middle of the street?" the old man shouted.

The garbage man climbed into his truck.

"Sorry. I wasn't thinking," he told the old man.

"So long," he told Delilah. "Thanks for the game."

"See ya," she said, and waved, and went on her way.

Bounce.

Delilah was dribbling her basketball to her house up the street.

Bounce.

She felt light, as if she were riding on a soft sighing wind.

Bounce.

She knew how to do lay-ups.

Oof....

DRIZZLE

When Saturday arrived with a bad case of the drizzles, Delilah came down with a bad case of the gloomies.

She did the only thing possible, under the circumstances. She took her drums, her drumsticks, and her gloomies—to the park.

It was dark and wet there. And empty.

"Perfect," said Delilah as she set up her drums.

BOOMBOOMBOOM.
BOOMDEBOOM.
BOOMBOOM BOOMBOOM.
BOOMDEBOOM.

She took a deep breath. For a second, the gloomies lifted. Then they fell around her again.

BOOMBOOM.
BOOMBOOMBOOM.
TCHICKADOOM.
TCHICKADOOM.
TCHICKADOOMDOOMDOOM.

She breathed deeply. The gloomies lifted a little more.

A worm came out to hear her play.

A squirrel scrambled down one tree and up another.

Delilah drummed for the worm
and for the squirrel.

TCHICKADOOMBOOMBOOM.
TCHICKADOOMBOOMBOOM.
BOOMTCHICK BOOMTCHICK.
BOOMDOOMBOOM.

Delilah smiled.
She felt a lot better.

So did the worm. He wiggled for more.

Delilah played him an encore. He wiggle-danced throughout. Delilah admired his sense of rhythm.

Next a brown bird joined in.

The bird sang. The worm danced. And Delilah drummed.

BOOMTCHICKA.
BOOMTCHICKA.
BOOMBOOMBOOM.
TWEETWEETWEETWEETWEE.
TCHICKABOOMBOOMBOOM.
TWEEBOOMBOOMTWEE.
TWEEBOOMTWEEBOOM.
ACHOO!

Delilah sneezed.

I must be catching a cold, she thought. *But, on the other hand, the gloomies are definitely gone.*

Feeling cheerful now, Delilah said good-bye
to the bird and the worm. And to the squirrel.

On her way home, the rain stopped, the sun
came out, and Delilah blew her nose.

BIRTHDAY

It was two weeks before her birthday, but Delilah already knew exactly what she wanted. The trick was to let her mother and father know without really telling them. If she told them, it wouldn't be a surprise. And she knew her mother and father loved surprises.

At dinner that night, she dropped them a hint.

"We're studying how sound works," she said. "I learned how you get sound out of a record player. It's very, very interesting."

"How?" her father asked.

Delilah explained.

"You're right," he said. "That's very, very interesting."

Several nights later, they all went shopping together. Delilah stopped at a record bin and began thumbing through it.

Her mother said, "We'll meet you in Housewares."

And left her thumbing.

A salesman came over.

"May I help you?" he asked Delilah.

"Just looking," Delilah said, and made her way to Housewares, where she found her mother and father buying garbage bags.

In the car on the way home, Delilah asked her father what his favorite kind of music was.

"All kinds," he said.

"I guess I like rock best," her mother said.

"Me too," said Delilah.

"OK. I get it," her father said.

Then he turned the car radio to a rock station.

Delilah wasn't so sure her father got it.

The next week she borrowed a record of *Peter and the Wolf* from the library.

"Why?" her mother asked.

"Because I like it," Delilah answered. "And I'm going over to Monica's to listen to it."

"Too bad you don't have your own record player," her mother said. "By the way, would you mind picking up a carton of milk on the way home?"

Delilah didn't mind at all. In fact, she was very happy. She was sure her mother had guessed what she wanted for her birthday.

Now all she had to do was wait. Which was very hard to do.

But finally her birthday arrived.

She got seven out of ten wrong on a spelling test. Because she couldn't pay attention. Then her teacher asked her a question she couldn't answer. Because she didn't hear it.

It would have been an awful day. Except it was her birthday.

When Delilah got home from school, her mother and father were waiting for her. They had come home from work early.

"Happy birthday, Delilah!" they said, both at the same time.

"Thank you," Delilah said, biting her lip. She could hardly stand the suspense.

"We have a present for you," her father said. "In your room."

Delilah dashed off to her room. When she got

there, she stopped short. She was very surprised.

Curled up on her bed was a puppy. Sleeping.

"Oh!" Delilah said.

The puppy opened his eyes and looked at
her, without raising his head.

Delilah loved him at once and forever. She
called him Hi-Fido.

GRANDMA

Every once in a while, Delilah's mother went away on a business trip. Delilah looked forward to those times. She loved to be alone with her father.

Sometimes Delilah's father went away on a business trip. That was fun, too. Delilah and her mother would have long talks about all sorts of things.

Once a year, Delilah's father and mother went away on a vacation together. Those were awful times. Those were the times that Grandma came to stay.

Right now was one of those times. Grandma was in the kitchen, making Delilah's breakfast, and grumbling about it.

"You don't have to do that, Grandma. I can make my own breakfast."

Grandma took two eggs out of the boiling water.

"Never mind. It's already done. Here."

"Thank you," said Delilah.

"Where are you going today?" her grand-mother asked.

"To David's house. To play."

"Like that?"

"Like what?" Delilah asked.

"In those dirty pants with the hole in the knee and those silly feet on the seat? You look like a charity case."

"I'm comfortable," Delilah said, with her mouth full of eggs. She was eating as fast as she could.

"Don't gobble your food," her grandmother answered.

"I couldn't help it. It was so good," Delilah said as she finished. She was trying to make the best of a bad thing.

"And don't talk with your mouth full," Grandma said.

"OK, Grandma," said Delilah. "See you later."

"Why don't you comb your hair, at least, before you go?" her grandmother asked.

"Why don't you leave me alone!" shouted Delilah, at the top of her lungs.

Her grandmother looked surprised at first. Then she started to cry.

Delilah looked surprised, too. Then she started to feel sorry.

"I didn't mean to shout, Grandma," she said softly.

Grandma continued to cry.

"Please don't cry," Delilah said.

Grandma stopped crying. But she wasn't ready to forgive Delilah.

"Being old isn't easy, Delilah," she said. "You'll see. When you get to be my age, you'll be just like me."

Delilah didn't believe it for a minute.

She knew she would be different.

But she didn't say so.

Instead she said, "I'm sorry, Grandma."

And she really was.

On the first day of spring, it was beautiful.
It made Delilah happy. It made her so happy
that she wanted to sing.

"Oh, what a beautiful morning," she sang as
she put on her favorite pair of jeans.

Her mother came rushing in from the kitchen.

"Delilah, what's wrong?" she asked.

"Nothing," Delilah answered. "It's a beautiful
day, and I was just singing about it."

"So that's what it was. I thought you were
in pain."

Delilah blushed.

"Delilah, I know it's not right for a mother to
be discouraging, but you *are* the *worst* singer

I've ever heard. If you must sing, please sing somewhere else. OK?"

"Somewhere else." Delilah sang the words sweetly.

"That's a very old joke," her mother said, but she laughed anyway.

And Delilah went out for a walk.

It *was* a beautiful day. It made Delilah happy. It made her so happy that, despite herself, she burst into song.

A policeman, passing in his car, screeched to a stop.

"Whatsa matter, kid?" he asked.

"Nothing," Delilah answered. "It's a beautiful day, and I was just singing about it."

"So that's what it was. It sounded like appendicitis!"

Delilah blushed.

"Kid, I don't know how to say this to you, but you're the worst singer I ever heard. You sing *terrible*."

"So I've been told," Delilah answered. "Sorry if I scared you."

"That's OK, kid. But if I was you, I wouldn't sing no more. Especially in public. So long."

And he took off.

It was still a beautiful day, but Delilah wasn't happy anymore. She wandered into the park and found a bench where she could sit and feel sorry for herself.

After a while, she heard a faraway sound. It was band music. Awful band music. The *worst* band music she had ever heard. She followed the sound.

Soon she arrived at a small band shell,
occupied by a small band.

There were six players, playing a tambou-
rine, a drum, a cornet, a trombone, and two
tubas. And there was a bandleader.

All of them must have been at least eighty-
five years old.

They called themselves the Golden Age Brass Band. At least, that's what it said on the back of the bandleader's jacket.

"Hi!" Delilah said when they'd finished their number.

"What'd ya say?" the bandleader asked her.

Delilah moved a little closer.

"I said hi."

"I didn't quite get it. Would you mind speaking up? A little hard of hearing, you know."

Delilah grinned.

"Can you play 'When the Saints Go Marchin' In'?" she shouted.

"Sure," the bandleader shouted back.

"Would you?" she asked.

"Of course," the bandleader said happily. It was the first time he'd ever been asked to play anything except somewhere else.

Delilah climbed onto the band shell.

"A-one, a-two, a-three, a-four," the bandleader counted.

And the band played.

And Delilah sang.

When they finished, they all clapped for each other.

"Do you know 'Hail, Hail, the Gang's All Here'?" Delilah shouted.

"Sure do," said the bandleader.

And, on the first day of spring, Delilah sang for joy.

GOOD NIGHT, SWEET DREAMS

Delilah loved to sleep. But she hated to go to bed.

Every night there came a time when her mother said, "Don't you think you ought to be getting to bed now?"

And every night, Delilah answered, "No."

"What about now?" her father would ask, three and a half minutes later.

"I just have to finish this chapter," she'd say, picking up a book and starting to read, very slowly.

"You're stalling," her mother would say after a time.

"This child needs reading lessons," her father might add.

Delilah would pretend not to hear them.

But the stubborn grin starting to grow on her face—just about then—would give her away.

"De—li—lah!"

That's all her mother would say. But she'd mean a lot more.

Delilah would know her time was up.

"Good night," she'd mumble, as she began the long, long walk to her bedroom.

She knew that as soon as she turned off her light and closed her eyes, the fun started outside. She didn't know exactly what kind of fun. But, then, how could she?

She always missed it.

One night Delilah's father came home with five free tickets to the circus.

Since he wanted to go, that left four tickets.

One of those was for Delilah, of course.

That left three.

Delilah's mother said she thought circuses were corny.

That still left three tickets . . . for three friends.

Delilah made a list in her head.

There's David and Claire and Monica and Bobby and Sally and Harry. One, two, three, four, five, six friends, she thought, and made a face.

"Your nose is wrinkled," her father pointed out.

"I know," said Delilah. "I have a problem."

"What's your problem?" her father asked.

"Six friends," Delilah answered.

"Not bad!" her father commented.

"And three tickets," Delilah added.

"I see," her father said. "Well, why don't your friends draw straws for the tickets?"

Delilah thought about it.

"I don't think it will work," she said.

"Why not? It seems fair."

She explained.

"They don't all get along," she said.

"You see, David thinks that Claire's a cry-

baby. And he's afraid of Bobby 'cause he thinks he's a bully. And he always says Harry's a yo-yo.

"So he won't go with any of *them*.

"But he likes Monica, Sally, and me.

"Now, Monica. She likes David, too. But she hates Sally.

"And Sally—she doesn't like Monica because Monica doesn't like her. And she thinks David's stuck-up.

"She does like Bobby and Harry and me.

"Now, Harry—Harry likes Bobby but he thinks Sally's full of baloney.

"Bobby likes Sally. But he agrees with David that Harry's a yo-yo.

"So I don't see how drawing straws can work.

"Phew!"

Delilah was very tired from figuring all that out.

"Let's give the extra tickets to the community center," her father suggested.

"Hundreds of kids belong to that," said Delilah. "How'll *they* figure out who should go?"

"I bet they'll find a way," said Delilah's father.

When Delilah and her father went to the circus, they sat with three children from the community center.

Everybody had a wonderful time and got sticky hands from the cotton candy. That is, everybody except David and Claire and Bobby and Harry and Monica and, of course, Sally.

It was Delilah's father's turn to make dinner. He was making fried chicken.

Delilah was helping him. She was making string beans.

Delilah's mother was taking a nap.

"We played basketball in school today. They made me captain," Delilah told her father.

Then she waited for him to say something nice—or something funny. She didn't care which.

"Oh," he said.

Just "Oh."

"Don't you think that's good?" she asked.

"Yeah, yeah. It's very good," her father answered.

But he didn't sound as if he meant it.

"Would you wake your mother and tell her dinner's ready?" Delilah's father asked, after a while.

Delilah tiptoed into her mother's room and sneaked up so close to her that their noses were almost touching.

"Dinner's ready, Mom," she whispered.

Then she waited for her mother to open her eyes. She knew she'd be surprised at first. Then, when she recognized Delilah, she would smile. It always worked that way.

But Delilah's mother kept her eyes closed, turned her head away, and said she'd be right there.

"She'll be right here," she told her father, and helped him bring out the food.

They all sat down to dinner. Nobody said anything to anybody.

Delilah couldn't stand it.

"The chicken's good," she said.

"Thanks," said her father.

Then came the quiet again.

They finished eating without another word.

"I'm going to watch television," Delilah said, jumping up from the table.

"Good," her mother said.

Delilah tried very hard to watch television, but she couldn't pay attention.

For the first time in her life, she decided to go to bed early.

But she couldn't fall asleep.

She tried lying on her stomach. Then on her side.

She switched to her back. Then she tried her other side.

She curled up.

She stretched out.

Nothing worked.

After what seemed like a very long time, she heard her parents. They were talking. She couldn't hear their words, but their voices sounded very angry.

She wanted to cry, but she wouldn't let herself. She just lay there with her eyes closed and a big lump in her throat that made it hard to swallow.

Then her door opened. It was her mother and her father, together.

"Delilah, are you awake?" her mother asked, softly.

"Yes," Delilah answered.

"We had an argument," her father said. "A silly one."

"But it's over," her mother said. "We love each other very much, and we love you very much, and...."

Now that it was over, Delilah couldn't hold it in anymore. She started to cry.

Then her mother started to cry. And her father. They all cried together.

Delilah had never felt happier.

Delilah Bush is just ten years old. But she likes to say she's going on eleven.

For her thirteenth birthday, she wants a minibike.

When she's sixteen, she wants to visit her cousin in California. By herself.

If she grows up tall enough, she wants to play center for the New York Knickerbockers.

If she doesn't grow up *that* tall, she'll play guard. Or else she'll play drums with her own rock band.

Tomorrow, she has to go to the dentist.